For Jessica

PUBLISHED BY RIP SQUEAK PRESS
AN IMPRINT OF RIP SQUEAK, INC.
23 SOUTH TASSAJARA DRIVE
SAN LUIS OBISPO, CALIFORNIA 93405

Library of Congress Control Number: 2005926909

ISBN-13: 978-0-9747825-0-8
ISBN-10: 0-9747825-0-5
Printed in China by Phoenix Asia
1 3 5 7 9 10 8 6 4 2

New edition edited and designed by Cheshire Studio

Don't miss the other books in this series:
THE ADVENTURE *and* THE TREASURE

To learn more about Rip Squeak visit
RipSqueak.com

RIP SQUEAK AND FRIENDS

Rip Squeak and His Friends

Written by **Susan Yost-Filgate**

Illustrated by **Leonard Filgate**

RIP SQUEAK PRESS ～ SAN LUIS OBISPO, CALIFORNIA

ONE MORNING the humans left the cottage, taking their suitcases with them. The house was *soooo* quiet.

Rip Squeak sat at his desk, daydreaming about having a great adventure. He started to scribble a note when suddenly the aroma of cinnamon made his stomach growl. He followed the sweet smell into the hall and found his sister, Jesse. Together they tiptoed toward the kitchen.

"Are you sure all the cats went too?" asked Jesse.

"Don't worry," Rip replied, sniffing the air.

That's when they heard the sound every mouse dreads . . .

Meeeooooowwww!

Jesse let out a terrified squeal and clutched her doll, Bunny.

"Be brave," Rip said to himself as he peeked around the corner and saw a kitten lying on the floor, sobbing.

"Exc-c-cuse me," Rip stammered. "M-m-my n-name is Rip Squeak."

The kitten looked at Rip with tears in her eyes.

"I'm Abbey," she said. "My family left without me and I'm all alone."

"You're not alone," Rip said soothingly. "My sister, Jesse, and I live here too."

Then Rip's stomach began to growl again. "Hey, are you hungry?" he asked Abbey. "I know where there's a cinnamon bun. We could share it."

"Oh, I love cinnamon buns!" Abbey exclaimed.

Jesse was by Rip's side. "Then you won't eat us?"

"Of course not!" Abbey said, shocked at the idea. "I would never eat my friends!"

After breakfast, Rip and Jesse crawled onto Abbey's back and they raced to the garden at the speed of kitten.

Once there they played together for hours, telling stories and chasing butterflies.

Suddenly the sky turned dark and it began to rain. "Oooh, I *hate* getting wet," Abbey declared, as she ran back to the cottage with her new friends holding on tight.

"I want to play in the rain," Jesse announced when they were safely inside. "Not me!" said both Rip and Abbey, as they shook off the raindrops. Jesse put on her raincoat and boots, grabbed an umbrella, and ran back outside.

Rip and Abbey looked out the window and watched Jesse as she happily splashed in the rain puddles.

"Oh, *no!*" Abbey gasped as she saw two cold glowing eyes looking out from the bushes, directly at Jesse.

"A cat!" Rip shouted. He frantically banged on the window, but Jesse was lost in her rain dance. She didn't see or hear a thing until the giant yellow tomcat slinked toward her.

Then Jesse surprised everyone. She used her umbrella to poke the bad cat right in the nose! But that wasn't enough to stop him. . . .

Then the strangest thing happened. A creature wearing a big hat and cape appeared out of nowhere, grabbed Jesse, and pulled out a sword. Totally confused, the enemy cat turned tail and ran.

"He almost got me, but I fought back!" Jesse said excitedly as she raced inside to her big brother.

"You sure did!" Rip agreed, hugging her close.

"All for one and one for all," the creature said. "Let me introduce myself. Call me Eur-ribbit-ribbit." He frowned and cleared his throat.

"Pardon me a moment. An actor must constantly practice the art of speaking clearly." His tongue began to flutter and his throat began to vibrate.

"Frrreckled frrrogs frrrolic frrreely," he recited several times.

Finally he grinned, took a deep bow, and said, "Call me Euripides!"

"Abbey," he asked, "are you going to introduce me to your friends?"

"This is Rip and Jesse," she said proudly.

"I've never met an actor," Rip confessed as he shook the frog's hand.

"Well, there is a first time for everything, Rip. I don't know about you, but I think we should all have something warm to drink. There's nothing like chamomile tea to soothe the nerves after such an ordeal."

They sat together for a long time, listening to Euripides tell stories about his life as an actor.

"You are a wonderful audience," Euripides suddenly announced, "but I'm afraid I must be off to the theater."

"It's still raining," Rip reminded him.

"Ah, my dear boy, the show must go on."

As Euripides was leaving, Abbey called after him, "What will we do for the rest of the day?"

"Use your imagination!" Euripides shouted. "Improvise!"

"What does that mean?" Rip asked.

"It simply means that you should make the most of an unexpected situation," he answered, and then vanished out the cat door.

"What do you think about having popcorn for
lunch? Is that a way to improvise?" Jesse wondered.

"It's a good start," Abbey and Rip agreed.

So they made popcorn, told silly jokes, and then played
a game of hide-and-seek. When it was Abbey's turn to hide, Rip and Jesse
couldn't find her anywhere.

Then they heard a melancholy sound coming from the living room and
found Abbey gingerly pressing the keys of the piano with her paws.

"What's wrong?" Rip asked.

"Oh, Rip . . . I miss my family!" said Abbey forlornly.

"Please don't stop playing, Abbey. Maybe if you play some happy music
it will make you feel happy too."

Rip's idea worked. Abbey cheered up and the sound of her beautiful music even drew Mr. and Mrs. Squeak into the living room.

Then there came a loud *thump* from the kitchen. Everyone froze, worried that it was the evil tomcat.

"I hope I haven't startled you," Euripides said as he entered the room. "Continue playing, my sweet girl. The matinee was a great success and I feel like singing happy songs!"

"I really don't know how to play anything else," Abbey said shyly.

Euripides hopped onto the piano. "Then we'll improvise!" he said as he started to sing in a booming operatic voice.

Rip started to dance on the keys. Abbey listened to Rip's tune and followed along with him.

"Lovely harmony!" Euripides said. "That's the spirit!"

In the midst of all the merriment, Abbey suddenly lifted her paws off the keyboard. The silence caught Rip and Euripides in mid-note.

"Are you alright?" Rip asked her.

"Oh, yes," she said with a big grin. "I've got a surprise for you."

"A surprise?" said Euripides. "Then I must change into something more appropriate."

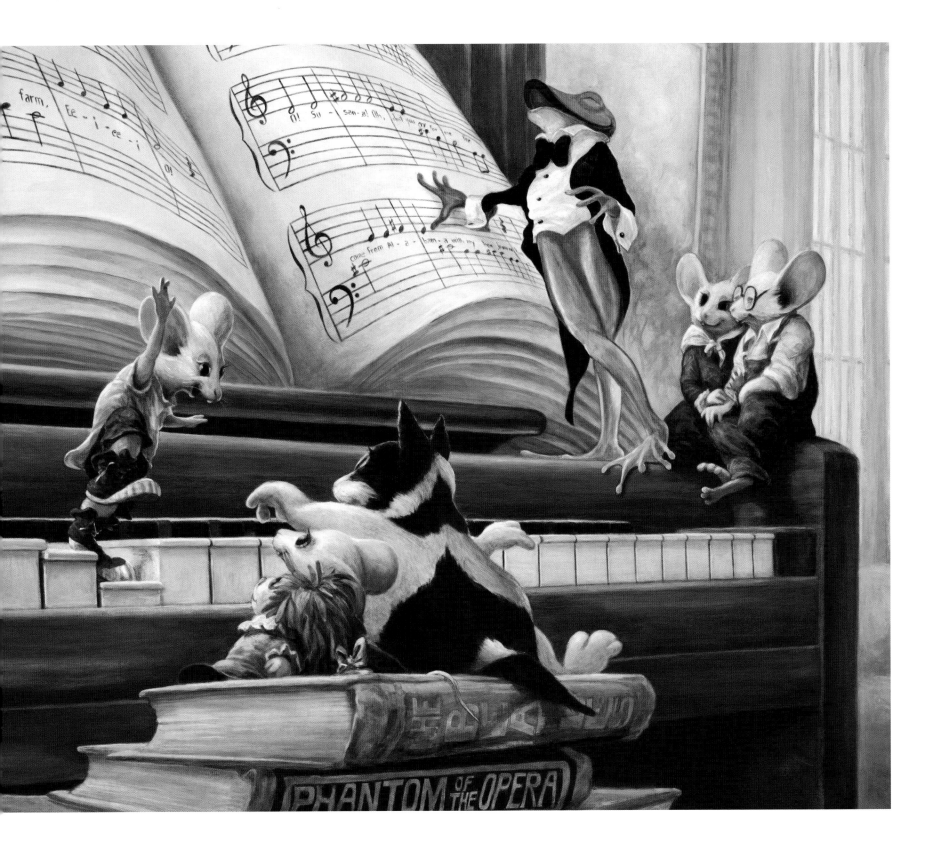

When Euripides returned, everyone wanted to know what he was this time. "Why, I'm a harlequin, of course."

"A whataquin?" Jesse asked.

"A harlequin. A jester. A fool. A clown," Euripides explained. "And now I am ready to go off on Abbey's adventure."

"All aboard," called Abbey, "and hold on tight."

She bounded up the stairs, stopping in front of a closed door.

"This is it!" she declared. Abbey let off her passengers and pushed open the door with one grand sweep of her tail.

Abbey's friends could not believe their eyes.
"So many toys," said Jesse in wonder.
"It's like Christmas!" Rip blurted gleefully.
"It is indeed!" said Euripides.
"I wanted to share this with you," Abbey said proudly. "You are the best friends—no, you're the best *family* anybody could wish for!"

"Let's play!" yelled Rip, running into the middle of the room.

"This marionette looks a lot like you, Euripides," teased Jesse.
"Did you already know about this place?"

Euripides laughed. "I wish I had known about this place my
dear girl. You'll learn that life is full of mysterious coincidences."

"Look at me," yelled Abbey, as she tried to balance herself on
a ball.

"We've discovered a whole new world," exclaimed Rip, "and
to think it was right under our noses the entire time!"

They played until they were too tired to play anymore.

Then they all wandered downstairs into the sunroom, where Abbey yawned and curled up on a plump pillow for a catnap.

Euripides, Jesse, and Rip nestled against her, and the sound of her soft purring lulled them to sleep.

As Rip's eyes grew heavier, he realized this day had changed everything. And when his eyes closed, he dreamed of the adventures tomorrow would bring.